Unlike any sheep or goats I'd ever seen...

Wow, this was really strange. I mean, we were hearing chanting voices coming from somewhere, yet we couldn't see anyone or anything that might have been the source.

Then...they appeared! We saw them marching in single file out of the bushes along the creek (Snort had called them "butches," remember?), the bushes along the creek, and you talk about getting a case of the CREEPS! The hair on the back of my neck shot up. My eyes bugged out and electricity crackled down my backbone and went out to the end of my tail, where it fried a clump of hair.

No kidding, *fried* it.

Here's what we saw: seven creatures unknown to us. They were tan in color, bigger than coyotes, bigger than mule deer, but smaller than cows or horses. They wore huge curled horns on their heads and each had a shaggy mane or beard flowing down the front of its neck.

They resembled sheep or goats, but unlike any sheep or goats I'd ever seen...

The Case of the Wandering Goats

John R. Erickson

Illustrations by Gerald L. Holmes

Maverick Books, Inc.

MAVERICK BOOKS, INC.
Published by Maverick Books, Inc.
P.O. Box 549, Perryton, TX 79070
Phone: 806.435.7611
www.hankthecowdog.com

First published in the United States of America by Maverick Books, Inc. 2017.

1 3 5 7 9 10 8 6 4 2

LIBRARY OF CONGRESS CONTROL NUMBER: 2017900738

978-1-59188-169-8 (paperback); 978-1-59188-269-5 (hardcover)

Dedicated to the grandchildren of
George and Dana Clay:

Jake Naus,
Logan Clay,
Avery Clay,
Luke Naus,
Lottie Cluy

CONTENTS

CHAPTER ONE

The Monkey Pirates

It's me again, Hank the Cowdog. It was a gloomy, dark night in May, as I recall. Yes, it was May, and as I paced the deck, I noted the location of every star. They were all overhead in the sky.

I felt uneasy. This was no ordinary gang of pirates we were after, but a crew of monkey pirates under the command of the notorious Captain Gooey Louie. They had captured a shipload of boiled turkey necks, and had spread fear up and down the coast of Menudo.

I was commanding a three-masted man-of-war, HMS Whickerbill, and the Admiralty had sent us around the Cape of Good Honk in pursuit of the pirates. My orders were to engage them in combat, eat the cargo, and sink the ship.

I made my way across the creaking deck and joined the young sailor who was steering the ship. In the hazy moonlight, he looked nervous and not very smart.

"How long have you been at sea, lad?"

"Murgle skiffer pork chop."

"That's a long time. I guess you're missing home."

"Mork snerk snicklefritz."

"I understand. This ocean is a huge place, and it's always full of water."

"Watery pottery slottery, the mouse ran down the clock."

"Oh? Set three traps and arm them with peanut butter. Steer a course south by southwest."

"Hank?"

"You may call me Captain."

"I hear someone coming."

I cocked one ear and listened. "You're right, it must be the monkeys. Draw cutlasses and prepare to board the ship!"

"Hank, you'd better wake up."

"What do you mean, 'wake up'?" I blinked my eyes and glanced around. Everything had changed. "Good grief, it's daylight and our ship has vanished! Where is the ocean? Why wasn't I informed?"

"Well, I guess we were asleep."

"Don't be absurd. I had the night watch and you…" I staggered a few steps and took a closer look at the sailor. "Who are you?"

"I'm Drover, remember me?"

"No. Wait. Did you say Drover?"

"Yeah, Drover with a D."

"You're the one with the stub tail?"

"Yeah, but I don't want to talk about it."

"Neither do I." I glanced around. We appeared to be in a room of some kind. "Drover, I don't want to alarm you, but there's a strange man over there, dressed in boxer shorts and a T-shirt. He's sitting in a chair. What's going on around here?"

"That's Slim. He's eating breakfast."

"He's eating a dead lizard?"

"No, it's a boiled turkey neck."

"Ah, of course, yes. He must have gotten it from the pirates."

"There aren't any pirates."

"No pirates? Wait, hold everything. Don't you get it? That's Slim Chance!"

"Yeah, that's what I said."

"Maybe we spent the night in his house."

"Duh."

"I beg your pardon?"

"I think you were dreaming about monkeys."

I glanced around, in case we were being watched. "Who told you that?"

"You did. You were babbling about monkeys and ships."

"Let's get one thing straight: I don't babble."

"You do when you're half-asleep. I heard you."

"Stop eavesdropping on me." The fog lifted and my head began to clear. "Okay, I'm seeing a pattern here. You're Drover. We spent the night at Slim's place and that's him sitting in the chair."

"That's what I said."

"Please don't interrupt. Did he offer us a bite of his breakfast?"

"Not yet."

"That's very slurp of him. Maybe we should..." My ears began picking up signals from outside. "Is that a vehicle?"

"Yeah, I tried to tell you."

"Why didn't you bark?"

He yawned. "It seemed like a lot of trouble."

"Drover, this is shocking, and please stop yawning. An intruder is approaching the house, and all you can do is yawn about it?"

"Well..."

"Battle stations! Load up guns one and two. Let's lay down some cover fire!"

We turned our big guns toward the front door

and began pumping out some heavy-duty barks. You should have been there to see it! It was an awesome display of...

"Hank, dry up!"

Huh? Had I heard a voice?

Yes, and it came again. "It's probably Loper, so knock it off."

Okay, that was Slim's voice and maybe our blasts of barking had disturbed his breakfast. How's a dog supposed to know? We just try to do our jobs, but speaking of breakfast, I left the artillery and made my way over to his chair. Maybe...

"No."

What a grouch. I hadn't begged for food. What kind of lunatic would eat a cold, leftover, boiled turkey neck for breakfast anyway? It looked revolting.

"You want a bone?"

No.

He pitched it in the air and, well, what could I do but snag it? Snarf. It crunched up pretty nicely. Turkey neck bones don't look so great and a lot of dogs wouldn't touch one first thing in the morning, but they're not all that bad.

Crunch, crack.

Pretty good in fact. Give me a choice between

a neck bone and a plate of scrambled eggs, and I'll take the bone every time. You know why? Because in Slim's house, a decent, civilized breakfast will never happen, so we take anything we can get.

As a matter of fact...

"That's all you get."

You see how he is? The man seems to think that a dog has only one thing on his mind and all we ever do is chase after the next meal. It's very discouraging and even insulting. For his information, the mind of a dog is an *awesome thing*.

The only reason dogs aren't listed among the world's greatest philosophers and poets and composers is that we're stuck with the job of protecting knot-heads like Slim Chance—for which we receive no credit or appreciation, only criticism and scorn.

Free us from that burden and see what happens. We'll write the great books, think the great thoughts, and compose the great slumphonies.

Timpanies. We'll compose the greatest timpanies ever heard.

That doesn't sound right. It drives me batty when the perfect word is right on the tang of my torque and I can't come up with it.

The word I'm searching for has to do with

fiddles and horns and a guy standing on a platform, wearing tusk and tails, and waving a little stick around.

Phooey.

You know what? I don't care and I'm not going to waste half my life looking for a word I don't care about. The important poink is that dogs need nutrition and energy, and we can't get it by eating sheet music.

We need FOOD, and would it drive the ranch into bankrubble if Slim shared one more turkey vertebra with his best friend in the whole world?

Was that unreasonable?

I mean, we ask so little of this life!

I unloosed a moan from deep in my throatalary region, moved my front paws up and down, and beamed him an expression of Adoration and Starvoration.

I studied his face. His mouth was stiff, cold, lifeless, without even a hint of warmth or compossem. This wasn't going to work. But wait...

There was a flicker of something...a softness came into his eyes...his lips stirred ever so slightly and the corners moved upwardly at the corners.

Holy smokes, IT WAS A SMILE!

"Okay, pooch, one more. See if you can catch it."

With his thumb, he flipped a vertebra high

into the air. I loaded the Reentry Data into the computer and moved into the Recovery Position. When the object began its downward plunge, I was waiting and snapped it right out of the sky.

Crunch.

Oh yes! The bonds of our bondage had bonded, and we were friends again, friends forever, friends to the bone!

A little humor there, did you get it? "Friends to the BONE," as in a turkey vertebra. Ha ha.

Anyway, he was pleased and proud. He not only smiled, he uttered a chuckle, and don't forget, this was early morning, not his best time of day. "Nice work, pup. You've got talent nobody ever dreamed was there."

Right. Did we have time for one more?

No, because at that very moment, we heard pounding at the door. Our pleasant episode came to a sudden end and I was back on duty.

"Symphony," that's the word I was looking for.

CHAPTER TWO

Police At the Door!

Bam, bam, bam!

I whirled around, did a quick-draw, and fired off three barks at the door. Drover uttered one squeak, dashed down the hall, and vanished in Slim's bedroom. The little weenie.

Slim remained in his chair. "Come in, Loper, it ain't locked!"

Loper? Okay, he was the boss, the guy who owned the ranch. I trotted over to the door and waited to clear him through Security. When the door swung open, I saw a man who wasn't Loper, not even close to being Loper.

I didn't know him, had never seen him in my entire life. He was dressed in a blue uniform with some kind of badge on the shirt pocket. He wore black Wellington boots and a felt cowboy hat, and...good grief, a thick black belt with a pistol on the right side!

He was armed! Was this one of the pirates? No, they were monkeys, so skip that.

I shot a glance at Slim. His mouth fell open and his eyes did too. Those were alarming signs. Just to be on the safe side, I scrambled away from the door and took refuge...that is, I set up a defensive position behind Slim's chair, where I could monitor the situation and fire off a few barks if necessary.

The stranger spoke. "Did I come at a bad time?"

"Bobby, whenever you show up is a bad time."

Hold everything. Bobby? That name had a familiar ring around the bathtub. A familiar ring, let us say. I had heard it before and maybe I knew the guy: Chief Deputy Bobby Kile. Remember him? You need to pay attention.

Okay, I knew him pretty well and we'd even worked some crinimal cases together. Remember the Case of the Monkey Burglar? We worked that one as a team and sent a crook to the slammer.

Wait, hold everything and check this out: monkey burglar and monkey pirates. Was this some kind of clue? No, never mind. Skip it.

Anyway, here he was—Deputy Kile, that is, not a monkey—standing in the door of Slim's shack at seven o'clock in the morning. And did I mention that he was holding some kind of big cooking pot? He was. What was going on around here?

Slim must have been wondering the same thing. "Well, you might as well come in. What's in the pot?"

"Lamb's quarter greens. We have a bunch of it growing in the shipping pens. My wife picked some and made a batch for you. She worries that you'll get scurvy, living alone out here in the Wild West."

Slim laughed. "Scurvy. Never even considered it. Set it in the kitchen."

Deputy Kile went into the kitchen and left the pot on the table. At that point, I noticed an important detail: he had a wad of chewing gum stuck to the seat of his pants. A dog notices those little details.

He came back into the living room and stared at Slim. "You dress like this all the time?"

"I wasn't expecting company at seven o'clock in the morning. When you show up without an appointment, you get what you deserve."

"Most of the people I know have already done

half a day's work by seven o'clock. What's wrong with your legs?"

"Nothing's wrong with my legs."

"They're pale, don't look natural, and awful skinny."

"I use 'em for walking around and they work just fine."

"What's that you're eating?"

"Turkey neck. I buy 'em ten pounds at a time and boil 'em up. They're better than you think. There's three more in the ice box if you want one."

The deputy made a sour face. "No thanks." He sat down in a chair and I went over to say hello. He rubbed me on the ears. "Morning, Hank." He glanced around the room. "Boy, times have really changed."

"What is that supposed to mean?"

"When I was a kid, going to the movies on Saturday, we never saw Roy and Gene dragging around the bunk house in their shorts. Back then, a cowboy was a hero, an example for the youth of America. It's kind of sad, the way things have gone downhill."

Slim nibbled on his breakfast. "You know, I was thinking the same thing about law enforcement. Back when Marshall Dillon was in charge of things, average tax-paying citizens never had to worry about a deputy banging on the door at seven o'clock in the morning. Bobby, what are you doing here?"

"I brought you a pot of greens. I thought you might be grateful."

"Bobby, what are you doing here? And you can skip the fluff."

The deputy's eyes roamed the ceiling. "I had a little favor to ask."

"That's what I figured. What?"

"How much do you know about goats?"

Slim gnawed the meat off another vertebra. "Hank, heads up." He flipped it in my direction and we're talking about a long shot, all the way across the room. I snagged it. Yes! Slim was pleased. "That dog ought to be playing college basketball. I don't know anything about goats and it makes me a happy that I don't. If I had to learn about goats, it would take brain space away from more important things. Why?"

"There's twelve head of 'em running a-loose on the creek."

"How'd you know that?"

"At 5:06 this morning, I got a call from your future daddy-in-law."

"Woodrow? Heh. He can't sleep past five o'clock, so he calls people."

"He said he had a herd of goats in his yard and they were eating Rose Ella's flowers. He and Viola tried to pen 'em, but they scattered."

Slim stared at him. "Good honk. Who owns goats around here?"

"The ag teacher bought 'em for the FFA kids at school. Something spooked 'em in the night. They tore down the pen and headed south. They're worth some money. They're show goats."

Slim gave that some thought. "I saw that movie when I was a kid, had some good songs in it. No, that was 'Show Boat.'" Deputy Kile groaned and shook his head. "But the point is that I've got work to do on the ranch. Remember back when you had an honest job? You had to get things done and earn your wages."

"I've already cleared it with your boss. He said getting you off the ranch for a day will improve everything."

"Sounds like something he'd say."

"I'll have to deputize you. Raise your right hand." Slim's right hand was holding the stub of a turkey neck and he didn't raise it. "Do you solemnly swear?"

"No."

"Too bad. You're in the County Militia. Here's your badge." He reached into his shirt pocket, pulled out a plastic badge, and pitched it to Slim. He caught it with his left hand and looked at it.

"Bobby, you ain't funny. I've told you that before."

The deputy laughed. "It came out of a box of cereal, but here's the deal. The school board wants the goats back and I need some help. And, frankly, you owe me."

"How do you figure that?"

"That day in the winter when your wheat pasture steers showed up on the golf course. Remember that? Your dog stole a hamburger from a lady at the Dixie Dog drive-in and the dogcatcher was fixing to haul him to the pound. Who bailed you out of that deal?"

"Maybe."

"And there's another way of looking at it." The deputy leaned forward and lowered his voice. "We might have to rope some of those goats."

Slim's eyebrows shot upward. "Well, why didn't you say that in the first place!"

"I've never tried to rope a goat, have you?"

"No, but I never let ignorance get in my way. I'll rope anything with hair. When do we start?"

"Right away, but Slim, there's one more thing." The deputy's face became very solemn. "You'll have to put on some clothes. When you ride for the County, you have to set a good example for the children."

They both laughed. "Bobby, you run a good joke right into the ground."

The deputy rose. "I'll go get my horse and meet you at headquarters at nine. Saddle your best roping horse and gather up all the pigging strings you can find."

Deputy Kile walked to the door and was about to leave, when Slim said, "Hey, Bobby?"

"What?"

"You've got chewing gum on the seat of your britches. It kind of tarnishes your image."

The deputy twisted around and looked. "Grandkids. I'll be there at nine, don't be late."

He left and Slim finished his breakfast. I, uh, sensed that he needed some help and sat down at his feet. See, I knew he still had some turkey bones sitting on the paper plate in his lap. Was there any chance...

"Where's Stub Tail? He might want some too. Drover?"

Stub Tail was hiding under the bed and didn't deserve any breakfast. I, on the other hand, had attended the entire meeting with Deputy Kile, and surely that was worth a bonus.

I licked my chops and squeezed up a Groan of

Desire. When Drover didn't appear, Slim shrugged. "Well, the world is run by them that shows up. Here, pooch."

He set the plate on the floor in front of me. It contained the last two turkey vertebrae and I had big plans for them.

But just then, Stub Tail came creeping out of the bedroom, and suddenly I faced a Moral Delemon. Would I share my stash of bones with him?

CHAPTER THREE

The Battle
of the Boots

S lim pried himself out of the chair, wiped his fingers on his shirt, and shuffled off to the bedroom to put on his clothes. Drover came padding over to me and saw the bones. "Oh goodie, I got here just in time."

"You got here just NOT in time."

He started bawling and collapsed on the floor, kicking all four legs. "No fair, I didn't get any breakfast!"

I ignored him and began crunching one of the two remaining turkey bones. I chewed it up and sent it down to the Department of Digestion, whilst the King of Slackers moaned and wailed.

"I never get any bones! How come you didn't save any for me?"

"Bones get eaten by those who show up. No show, no bones. You left the room and hid under Slim's bed."

He stopped crying and sat up. "How'd you know I was under the bed?"

"Because I know you. When you can't flee to the machine shed, you dive under the nearest bed. You're as predictable as water."

"How's water predictable?"

"Number one, it's always wet. Number two, it always flows downhill."

"Yeah, and it never walks. It always runs."

"Exactly my point. When you leave water running, it runs downhill. It follows the Laws of Gravy and its behavior is entirely predictable."

"Yeah, it runs but it never runs out of breath. Who could predict that?"

"What?"

"Well, when I run, I get tired and run out of breath, so I'm more predictable than water. And I love gravy."

I stared into the caverns of his eyes. "Okay, you're more predictable than water and you love gravy. I'm not sure where this is taking us."

His gaze went to the plate and he licked his chops. "There's one bone left."

"That has nothing to do with water or gravy."

"Yeah, but maybe you'd share it anyway."

I paced a few steps away. This was a tough decision because...well, because an element of confusion had crept into our conversation. We seemed to be arguing about something, but I wasn't sure *what*.

I paced back to him. "All right, you can have the bone...if you'll admit that you were wrong."

"About what?"

"I don't care. Pick something to be wrong about, admit it, and let's get on with our lives."

"Okay, I was wrong about the gravy."

"And you're sorry?"

"Oh yes."

"Fine. Try to do better next time, and you may eat the bone."

"Oh goodie, here I go!"

He pounced on the bone and began crunching. It made me proud that I had been so kind and generous to a friend, and that it had brought so much pleasure into his hollow little life.

But you know what? I couldn't shake the feeling that he was the weirdest little mitt I'd ever mutted...the weirdest little mutt I'd ever met, let us say. Did any of that conversation make sense to you? It didn't to me: running water, gravy. Wow, that was strange.

But at least he'd admitted that he was wrong, and that's very important in the overall scheme of things. When we're sure the other guy is wrong, it makes everything a lot simpler.

Anyway, Drover got his bone, whether he deserved it or not, and Slim put on his clothes, and we were ready for the day. Slim went to the closet and brought out his riding boots with the spurs attached. He always looks happy when he pulls on those boots, even though they're a tad too small and he always has to grunt and struggle to pull them on.

Why did he look happy? Because when he pulls on that special pair of boots (handmade by a guy in Amarillo, by the way), he's like a knight putting on his shining armor. It announces to the world that he's fixing to get ahorseback and do what cowboys love to do.

They don't love mowing weeds, driving the tractor, building fence, fixing windmills, or cleaning out the machine shed. They love climbing into the saddle and feeling the power of a good horse between their legs, taking hold of a pair of soft, oiled reins, and hitting a nice trot across big empty country.

And don't forget that Deputy Kile had mentioned *roping*. That really brought fire to

Slim's eyes, because he was what some people call a "Roping Fool."

He loved to rope and he was pretty good at it. He'd squandered hours of his life pitching his loop at roping dummies, bales of hay, and five-gallon buckets. He could catch heads, horns, or heels. He'd hauled his horse to ranch rodeos and team ropings all the way from Lubbock to Dodge City, and he'd won almost enough prize money to pay for his gas.

He'd never stuck his loop on a deer, elk, or cougar, but only because he'd never gotten the chance. He roped a badger once and learned a powerful lesson: it's a really stupid thing to do. The badger ran up the rope and offered to eat his horse. The horse sold out and the badger kept the rope.

I saw it. Really dumb.

Anyway, he was a certified Roping Fool and here he was, putting on his beloved riding boots. He got his left foot into the left boot (that was an important detail, left foot in left boot) and was straining to pull on the right one. That was the one that always gave him trouble, and it was giving him trouble now. With the fingers of both hands locked into the pull straps, he strained and grunted and hopped around on one leg.

I stood nearby, watching and cheering him on, as dogs have been doing for centuries. "Come on, cowboy, you can do it! Put your heart into it, heave ho!"

The last thing I expected was that he might hop into ME, but he did, and we're talking about bashing right into the middle of me. Oof!

"Look out, dog, I've lost my steering!"

I moved to the center of the room and staked out fresh ground. Good grief, he was coming toward me again, hopping like a maniac on a pogo stick! I tucked up my tail, did a one-eighty, and dived beneath the coffee table.

Drover was already there. He grinned. "Oh, hi. Thanks for the bone."

"How was it?"

"Pretty good, but it hurt my teeth. What's going on out there?"

"He's having trouble pulling on his boots."

We heard a crash. "Gosh, what was that?"

I peeked out of the bunker. "He fell. He's on the floor and still pulling. He needs our help. Come on!"

I dived out of the bunker and rushed to his side. Drover was right behind me, and began spinning around in circles. And squeaking. Slim was lying on his back now, with his right leg high in the air, and his face had turned red from the strain.

I moved right into the center of the crisis and began laying down Attaboy Licks to his nose. It worked. The boot finally slid into place and he climbed back to a standing position. He wiped his nose with the back of his hand and grumbled, "I might need to invest in a pair of thin socks. Let's go."

We got no thanks for our efforts and no credit for solving the Boot Problem, but that came as no surprise. Dogs ride for the brand and we let others take the glory, but let me point out something

about Slim and his boots. You won't learn this kind of stuff if you read the regular books and articles about the West, because they don't give the dogs' side of the story. If they did...wow.

I mean, a cowboy rolling around on the floor, trying to pull on his boot? We see crazy stuff like that all the time, every day, but you'll never read about it in the history books. If you want to know what REALLY goes on, ask the dogs.

I don't mean to get carried away, but these things need to be said and the cowboys aren't talking.

Where were we? Oh yes, those pirates. They were hauling a whole shipload of boiled turkey necks...wait, that was a bogus report. Just skip it. In fact, let's forget it ever came up. It wouldn't do the Security Division any good if...I mean, our enemies could do a lot of damage with that kind of gossip.

We must think of the morale of the unit. I'm sure you understand. Thanks.

Where were we? Oh yes. Slim had finally won the Bottle of Beets...the Battle of Boots, that is, and was back to walking upright on two legs. He grabbed his chaps and hat and we left the house.

Drover and I followed him to the pickup and

loaded up. I took the Shotgun Position and hung my head out the window. Drover whined about it but I ignored him. When he's old enough to handle the Shotgun Position, we'll think about giving him a promotion, but for now, he lacks training and experience.

His training and experience have made him an expert at whining about everything you can imagine. That might get you the Shotgun Position on some ranches, but not this one.

I have to set standards and be firm with the men, otherwise this place would go to pot.

So, yes, we started our two-mile drive to ranch headquarters, with me occupying the crucial Shotgun Position and Drover moping because he wasn't able to hang his head out the window and let the wind blow his ears around. At the mailbox, Slim made the usual right turn onto the county road and we headed west.

We had gone, oh, maybe a hundred yards when something darted across the road in front of us—two somethings, in fact. They were white and four-legged, quicker than raccoons and badgers, smaller than deer but bigger than rabbits.

I turned to Slim. He'd seen them too, and he said, "Well, there's two of Bobby's goats."

Goats? Oh yes, the goats, of course, just as I had suspected. We had hardly begun our morning's work, yet already I had located two of the wandering goats. That's the kind of success you can expect when you put the right dog in the Shotgun Position.

CHAPTER FOUR

A Mysterious
Buzzard Wing

Okay, put your books away and get out a sheet of notebook paper. We're going to have a pop quiz. And don't cheat. Ready?

Question: *When we arrived at ranch head-quarters, no dogs came out to bark at us. Why?*

Write down your answer and pass your papers to the front. The correct answer will be posted at the bottom of this page, and I must warn you, it's written in Secret Backwards Code.*

(Hint: If you hold your book in front of a Secret Backwards Mirror, it will appear in the normal unbackwards manner. Why? I have no idea. It's some kind of trick that mirrors can do and dogs don't understand, but CATS DON'T UNDERSTAND IT EITHER. That's a very

Because we dogs were riding in the pickup.

impointant pork.)

Did you get the right answer? I know this is pretty tough, but if we don't push ourselves, nobody will pull the wagon and we'll end up with the horse in front of the donkey. Standards will plummet and we'll all be standing around saying, "Duhhhhhh!"

Is that the kind of world you want to live in? Good. Neither do I, so study your lessons, eat lots of spinach, and brush your teeth every month.

Every day, that is. In fact, brush after every meal, and make sure you don't get spinach caught in your teeth, because people will stare at you and whisper, and your mother will scream.

She'll think your teeth are falling out.

Where were we? Oh yes, we arrived at ranch headquarters, and no dogs from the Security Division rushed out to bark at us, for reasons that you've already figured out. While Slim hooked up the stock trailer and went to the corral to saddle a horse, I hurried down to the yard.

You probably wonder what was the big deal at the yard that made me hurry. One word explains it: the cat. Actually, that's two words, but the main word is only one word and who cares if it's "a cat" or "the cat" or "some cat." The catness of a cat was the big deal, and I was fixing to get to the root of the carrot.

We're talking about Pete, of course, the local cat. There was no great mystery about where I would find the little sneak: lurking in the iris patch. He's too lazy to catch mice or do anything constructive on the ranch, so he sits around all day, lurking in the iris patch on the shady side of the house.

Actually, he wasn't in the iris patch on this occasion, and that confused me at first, but then I figured it out. Sally May, our Beloved Ranch Wife, had come out of the house and was standing at the yard gate. Kitty had pried himself out of the flowerbed so that he could rub on her legs, purr, meow, and make a nuisance of himself.

In that department, Nuisancing, he was Champion of the World.

Have we discussed my Position on Cats? Maybe not. I don't like 'em, never have, just have no use for a cat.

So what was Sally May doing at the gate? I didn't know and it didn't matter. What mattered was that Kitty was rubbing dandruff all over her jeans and tripping her every time she took a step, and someone needed to put a stop to it.

The very instant I rumbled up to the gate, I heard his whiny voice. "Well, well! It's Hankie the Wonderdog and you arrived just in time."

I hate that whiny voice. It makes my bloid bud...it makes my bud broil...it makes my blood boil, there we go. It doesn't matter what he says, it makes my boil bleed.

And you know what? It's not an accident. The little snot knows that his voice has an incendiary effect on my so-forth. We're talking about pitching gasoline on a campfire, and he uses it to provoke me into awkward situations.

The only reason it doesn't work is that I carry Iron Discipline in my kit of tools. It's a standard procedure in the Security Business, and we use it all the time on our Cat Calls. When we get a Forty-Twenty (that's the code for a Cat Call), we load up Iron Discipline and hit Sirens and Lights.

That's exactly how I arrived at the gate, armed with Iron Discipline and lights flashing. Kitty was rubbing all over Sally May's legs and smirking, of course. Always smirking, that's Pete. I've come to expect it and don't let it bother me.

Okay, it bothers me. In fact, it drives me nuts, but I don't let it bother me.

Anyway, when I rumbled up to the scene, my body had become a flashing electric arrow, pointing straight at Kitty. I had blotted the rest of Life Itself out of my mind, and heard an onimous rumble working its way up from the depths of my deeps.

I stuck my nose in his cheating little face. "Back off, Kitty, leave her alone, scram. She doesn't like you, nobody does, and she doesn't need cat hair all over her jeans. Move!"

Did he take the hint? Of course not. Cats are physically, mentally, and morally incapable of taking a hint. He threw a hump into his back and HISSED at me.

Oh, that did it! I hit Train Horns and blew him three steps backward. BWONK!

"Hank, stop it!"

Huh?

Okay, she was glaring down at me, Sally May that is, and maybe there was a note of irritation in her voice. Anger. Gee, what had I done?

She held something with feathers pinched between her finger and thumb. "Is this some of your work?"

My work? What was that? I moved toward it and turned on Sniffatory Scanners. Gag! WHAT WAS THAT? It smelled awful, and it looked awful too, like...I don't know, like a dead bird or something.

She leaned toward me and punctured me with an icy glare. "This is the wing off a dead buzzard!

How did it get here, right in the middle of the gate where everyone has to see it and smell it?"

Well, I...I had no idea. None. Honest. This was shocking. Who would do such a thing?

Wait. Okay, it was coming back to me. Last evening, before we left for Slim's place, I'd been checking things out along the creek and stumbled upon this Thing with feathers. The womenfolk are fond of feathers and flowers and pretty things, don't you know, and...well, my thoughts never stray far from Sally May.

Don't forget, one of my highest ambitions in life is to become The Dog of Her Dreams.

Last evening, in the soft twilight, I had noticed the pretty feathers and thought she might...I didn't pay much attention to the smell, which was kind of hard to believe, because, well, it really stank. That was obvious here in the light of day.

Anyway, I had carried it up to the house and left it for her at the yard gate. Hey, it was a *gift*. I didn't do it for myself, I did it for her, hoping it might win me a few points.

"Stop dragging dead things up to my yard!"

Well, this deal had gone south on me. My head sank. I switched on Looks of Deepest Remorse, and went to Slow Taps on the tail section.

"Sally May, I know this looks bad, and yes, it smells even worse. I find myself at a loss for words. I can't explain it, I mean, here, now, today it seems crude and outrageous. I can only say that, last evening, somehow it reminded me of YOU."

Would it sell? Would it help to heal the wound? Would we ever be able to repair the damage and patch up our relationship?

Holding the thing out at arm's length and wearing a horrible pinched look on her face, she headed for the trash barrel. Oh, and she was muttering. "Nasty dog! I can't believe he'd...oh!"

If you've never been a dog, you just don't

understand how hard it is to be a good dog. I mean, we try SO HARD to please our people, then something like this comes along and...it's very discouraging.

I was in the midst of these depressing thoughts when my gaze slid to the left and I saw the cat, licking his front paw with long strokes of his tongue. And I became aware of a detail that you probably missed, because...well, because you weren't there.

But I was there and I noticed it right away: Sally May had gone down to the trash barrel and left me alone with her rotten little cat.

We were on opposite sides of the yard fence—he on the inside, me on the outside—but here's the detail you missed:

Sally May had left the GATE OPEN.

Hmmm.

Women can be very subtle, you know. Was there a possibility that she...I cast a glance to the south. She had pitched the buzzard wing into the trash barrel and was now preoccupied with something else, pulling weeds.

Hmmm.

CHAPTER FIVE

Another Misunderstanding With Sally May

M y gaze slid back to her rotten little cat. "Hey Pete, has it occurred to you that we're sitting here, just me and you, all alone?"

He stopped licking himself and glanced around. "You know, Hankie, I hadn't noticed that, but we are."

"Had you noticed that she walked away and left the gate wide open?"

He studied the space left by the open gate. "Hankie, you're right about that. Good eye."

I rose to my feet and moved a few steps closer. "She's busy."

He looked off toward the south. "She is busy."

"Her broom is inside the house."

He gave that some thought. "I'll wager you're

right about that too, Hankie. She keeps it inside the house, beside the back door."

"Exactly. One more detail: there's a tree in front of the house."

His eyes grew wide. "Ohhhh, I see where this is going. You're wondering if I'd like to climb the tree?"

"Heh heh."

"It's not on my schedule, Hankie."

"Yeah, well, things come up all of a sudden."

He studied me for a long time with his yellow, scheming kitty eyes, then shrugged. "Sure, why not? It might be fun."

Huh? This caught me by surprise. "What is that supposed to mean?"

"Well, I'll get some exercise, which I hate but need, and you'll dig yourself an even deeper hole with Sally May."

"She's not watching. I'll have just enough time to park you in the tree and make my escape. She'll never suspect a thing."

He shook his head and laughed. "Oh, Hankie, you're something special! Very well, who goes first? Should I lead off with some hissing, or do you want to open things up with barking? Either way is okay with me."

There was something about this that made

me suspicious. I mean, the little creep seemed a little too comfortable with the idea of me chasing him up a tree. I paced a few steps away and sent an urgent message to Data Control. I needed help on this. Seconds later, I got a response.

She has radar.
She knows what you're thinking before you do.
If you don't believe it, look at her.

That was the message, so I, uh, moved my gaze in a southward direction and saw...oops, she had stopped pulling weeds and had parked her hands on her hips (always a bad sign) and was glaring straight at ME, and we're talking about Laser Vision.

Gulp. Okay, sometimes we get so caught up in the excitement of a concept, we forget certain deep and fundamental realities about Reality. The woman had radar for dogs. That was all I needed to know.

I paced back to the cat. "I'm calling it off. It's a no-go."

"Well, darn!"

"I don't have time for your silly little games this morning. I'm a very busy dog."

"Oh really. How exciting. Something major, I guess."

"It's an important case, highly classified. I'm not at liberty to reveal that it involves goats."

"Oh, then we mustn't talk about it. Shhh."

"Don't shush me. I'm in charge here."

"Sorry, Hankie, but I understand that we can't say a word about the goats."

"Exactly." There was a long moment of silence. "Did you say goats?"

"Me? Oh no, not at all. I said nothing about goats."

The hair rose on the back of my neck and I leaned closer to him, exposing two rows of fangs.

"HANK, LEAVE THE CAT ALONE!"

Huh? Good grief, I hadn't even touched the little snot. You see what I mean? No dog is safe around that woman. I, uh, took a step backward and melted my fangs into a pleasant smile.

"Pete, I don't mean to argue, but you *did* say something about goats. How did you get that information?"

"Well, Hankie, to be honest...you know, I hate being honest, but oh well. You let it slip."

"I did? That's impossible."

He shrugged. "Whatever you think, Hankie, but while I'm in an honest mood, I'll tell you something else." His creepy yellow eyes popped wide open. "I saw your goats this morning at first light. They were standing on a little hill north of the house."

"No kidding?"

"Yes, but they weren't goats, Hankie. They were Aoudad *sheep*. Did you know we have Aoudads on this ranch?"

"Of course I did. Who or whom do you think is in charge around here? But just for the record... what's an Aoudad?"

"Barbary sheep. They were brought over from North Africa."

"See? I knew that. Give me a description."

"Big. Shaggy. Tan. They have magnificent curled horns."

"How many?"

"Horns or sheep, Hankie?"

"Sheep."

"Seven, all standing in a line."

This time, it was my turn to laugh, and we're talking about a really wicked laugh of triumph. "Ha ha ha. Sorry, Kitty, won't sell. Lies never sell."

"But Hankie..."

"Number one, we're looking for goats, not sheep. Do you know the difference between a goat and a sheep? Of course not. Sheep make wool, Pete, and cats try to pull it over the eyes of others, but not today, not on this outfit."

"That's cute, Hankie."

"Number two, goats are white, small, and not shaggy. They have floppy ears and don't have 'magnificent curled horns,' to quote from your bogus report. Number three, we're looking for twelve goats, not seven sheep. Now that I've absolutely destroyed your testimony of lies," I gave him a warm smile, "do you have any questions?"

Wow, I had blown him off the map, but...hmm, he continued to smirk, and that bothered me for a moment. Then it came to me: when you're a dumb little ranch cat, what can you do but smirk? They smirk when they win and they smirk when they lose, and they're too dumb to know the difference.

The point is that I had mopped the floor with him and left him speechless...well, speechless until he was finally able to say, "One question, Hankie. Have you ever seen an Aoudad?"

"No, Kitty, nor have I seen a unicorn or a purple rooster, and neither have you, because they don't exist. The prosecution will rest its case." I whirled around and marched out of the courtroom, leaving the little sneak sitting in the ruins of his castle of lies. Hee, hee!

But wait! I whirled around and marched back

to him. I had one more thought to share. I put my nose right in his face and gave him Train Horns, and we're talking about a blast of righteous barking that pasted his whiskers all over his cheating little face!

Hee hee! Oh, how I love doing that!

WHAP!

Didn't expect the little pestilence to slap me across the nose. This meant war, total war, no prisoners, Kitty up a tree!

"HANK, LEAVE THE CAT ALONE!"

Huh?

As I've said many times before, and I hope the children will pay attention here, when you win in a court of law, you don't need to climb into the gutter with all the cats and rats and guttersnipes. You win through logic and reason, and it doesn't get any better than that.

Once again, I had won a huge moral victory over the stupid cat, and marched away from the...phooey.

CHAPTER SIX

Locked In A Dungy Dingeon!

Kitty was the World Champ of the cheap shot, and if he hadn't lived under the constant protection of Sally May's mind-penetrating radar, he would have been a greasy spot on the prairie long ago.

My nose hurt like crazy, but the important thing to remember is that I didn't care. I had chosen to devote my life to the defense of Higher Things, and that was a reward in itself.

Think about it. In his old age, when Pete was too feeble to cheat and cheap-shot, he would have nothing to share with his grandkitties except dreary stories about his career as a bragging, boasting, lie-infested, cheap-shot artist. Nothing good or noble.

It was kind of sad, really. Even so, he would pay.

I made my way up the hill to the machine shed, and there I encountered Guess Who. Apparently he had been sitting in the same spot, doing nothing since we had arrived at headquarters with Slim.

When he heard my footsteps approaching, his dreamy gaze drifted down from the clouds. "Oh, hi. Where have you been?"

"I've been trying a case in court."

"I'll be derned. How'd it go?"

"Great, we blew 'em away."

"What happened to your nose?"

"Nothing happened to my nose, and don't be spreading lies."

"It's got red spots."

"Oh, those? Yes, I won such an awesome victory over the cat, I broke out in hives of joy."

"Bees do that all the time."

"What?"

"They get hives and make honey."

"That's true, good point."

"I heard a noise. It sounded like a woman yelling."

"Maybe she was stung by a bee."

"No, she said something about a cat."

"Maybe the cat was stung by a bee. I hope so."

"I think it was Sally May. Did you get in trouble again?"

I melted him with a glare. "Yes, if you must know, I got in trouble, and for sticking your nose into my business, you get five Chicken Marks."

"I guess you stuck your nose into Pete's business and got slugged."

"Ten Chicken Marks."

"Hee hee."

"Twenty! This will go into your record."

"Deputy Kile is here."

"Thirty! What did you say?"

"Me? Gosh, I don't remember."

"Drover..."

"Wait, here we go. Deputy Kile is here."

"Why wasn't I informed?"

"Oh, you were too busy getting in trouble, I guess."

"They'll need my help with the goats." I pushed him aside. "Get out of my way, stop talking about bees, and go to your room."

I left him sitting there with a vapid grin on his face. You see what I have to deal with in this job? My assistant is a nincompoop and it's almost impossible for me to get any work done. If he's not whining about Life's injustice (the Shotgun Position in the pickup), he's spreading lies and

gossip about his superiors.

Or jabbering about bees and honey. Where did that come from? I have no idea. Sometimes I think...

You know what Drover needed more than anything? A quick court martial that would land his nose in the corner for two solid hours. Yes sir. If there was any help of hoping him, that was it. Hope of helping him, it should be, but I'm not sure there was any help of hoping him. Hope of...

This is what he does to me, he and Sally May's rotten little cat, but their times were coming, oh yeah. When I got the Goat Deal straightened out, Drover would stand with his nose in the corner for hours, and Kitty would be parked in the nearest tree.

Aoudad sheep. Dumbest thing I'd ever heard.

Of course there was another way of viewing Drover's weirdness. Maybe...maybe I'd been too hard on the little goof. I mean, let's face it, the Lottery of Life hadn't been kind to him. He'd ended up with the heart of a chicken and a ridiculous stub tail, and those of us with stout hearts and long handsome tails...well, there's no way we can understand how it would be to wake up every day with a chicken's heart and a tail that made everyone in the room double over with laughter.

And don't forget his bad leg. Hey, that leg had caused him terrible suffering over the years. I knew because I'd been there to see it, and I'd witnessed his allergy attacks too, when the poor little guy was snorting and honking, and all he could say was, "By dose is stobbed ub."

Sorry, I didn't mean to load you down with all the Burdens of Leadership. When your name is at the top of the list, this is what you get: everyone's problems, everyone's weird little habits.

You know what Drover really needed? Not a corner to put his nose in, but a friend, someone who would listen and share and understand. All at once, I was ashamed of myself. What a heartless cad I'd been!

I did a one-eighty and went back to give the runt some sympathy and counseling.

Hmm, he had vanished. Gee, maybe I'd broken his heart and he'd gone to some dark place to cry out his sorrow.

I felt a growing sense of regret. How could I have been so...but then I heard voices and saw him...huh? I saw him down at the yard gate. He seemed to be talking with...THE CAT!

I lifted Earoscanners and listened.

DROVER: "Boy, you sure messed up his nose."

KITTY: "Yes, well, he was being his usual cloddish, overbearing self and needed some tutoring."

DROVER: "Tutoring. Oh, that's wicked!"

KITTY: "Of course, hee hee, I knew Sally May was watching."

DROVER: "Yeah, he never seems to figure that out. Hee hee."

Anyway, as I was saying, Drover is the King of Slackers and a shameless hypocardiac, and when I got the Case of the Wandering Goats wrapped up, his court martial would be at the top of my list of things to do.

And Kitty? He would get himself parked so high in the tree, we might not see him again for weeks. If Sally May wanted to dote over the little mutter mumble, she would need an extension ladder to do it.

Ha! So there!

I lifted my head to a proud angle and marched down to the corrals. Chief Deputy Kile had arrived, and had changed into his work clothes: jeans, denim shirt, boots and spurs, and a straw hat. He and Slim were loading their horses into the ranch's sixteen-foot gooseneck trailer.

Good. Even without my help, they were moving things in the right direction.

Slim saw me and said...I might have mis-understood. I thought he said, "Oh great, it's Bozo."

I marched up to them and gave a crisp salute. "Great news, men. I'm here! Are we ready? Let's get cracking."

I waited for...well, for some kind of greeting or response. They said nothing, just exchanged long glances. Then Slim walked into the corrals and called my name. "Come on, pooch!"

Actually, "Pooch" wasn't my official name, but that's what he called me most of the time, and that was okay. Good friends often use nicknames. It's a sign of affliction.

Affection, that is. It's a sign of infection and loyalty.

I slithered my enormous body under the bottom two-by-six board in the corral fence and followed him to the feed shed. He opened the door and pointed inside. "Check for mice, Hankie."

Aye aye, sir! I dashed inside and went straight to five bales of prairie hay that were stacked against the west wall. That's where the mice hung out, beneath those bales. I switched on Snifforadar and went to work.

Sniff, sniff.

Soon, the signals were pouring in. Yep, we had mice all right, several of them, and if Slim would start moving the bales...hmmm, the light in the shed had dimmed because, well, the door had closed.

Okay, the wind must have blown it shut, but...I glanced around...where was Slim? Apparently he'd been outside when a gust of wind had blown the door shut, but he would figure it out in a second.

I waited. That has always been hard for me, you know, waiting. After you've spent a few years in the Fast Lane, you find it hard to go back to the boring rhythms of ordinary life.

I found myself losing patience. "Hey, we've got goats to catch! You guys might have all day to goof off, but some of us have schedules to keep." I cocked my ear and listened. Nothing, not a sound.

Wait, there was a sound, a kind of thudding noise...two of them, almost as though someone had, well, slammed the doors of a car. Or a pickup.

A motor started. A vehicle seemed to be driving away. What was going on around here?

I glanced around and barked. "Slim? Enough of this! We've got an important case ahead of us and we need to start on it right away, before those goats...Slim? I'm not kidding about this. Open the door and let me..."

Then it hit me like a bag of cement dropped

from the sky. They had gone off and left me in a dingy little feed shed, while they drove off to have all the fun!

What a cheap trick! I couldn't believe it. Okay, Sterner Measures, by George. I grabbed a big gulp of carbon diego, fired up engines one and two, and rammed my entire body into the... BLAM...door, but some scrounge had latched it shut from the outside.

Ouch. I picked myself off the floor and glanced around at the place that had become my prison cell. All my life's hard work and training had come down to THIS, locked away in a dungy dingen while my former friends went off to chase goats!

Oh, treachery! Oh, broken dreams!

It looks hopeless, doesn't it? But don't give up just yet. See, there was one small detail...you'd better keep reading.

CHAPTER SEVEN

I Arrest An Intruder

Okay, where were we? Oh yes, all the so-forths of my so forth had come down to this, locked away in a dingy prison cell, tossed away like an old grease rag into the Garbage Heap of Life.

Is that cruel or what? I mean, we dogs ride for the brand and give 'em the best years of our lives, and this is the thanks we get.

But there was a tiny detail you missed. Do we dare reveal it? Might as well, sure, because if we don't, this story will become a dead duck, so pay attention.

If you recall, I had spent time in this particular feed shed on several occasions. Remember *The Case of the Tricky Trap*? Great story. On a dark night, I caught one of our local hoodlums inside the shed, ripping open feed sacks and scattering pellets of cow feed.

His name, of course, was Eddy the Rac, a typical thieving, barn-wrecking raccoon, only Eddy was even more typical than most coons. He was pretty smart and pretty tricky, though not half as smart and tricky as he might have thought. See, he came smack up against ME and that put a whoa to his crinimal mischief.

Hey, I don't take trash off the cats and I don't take trash off a coon either. I raided the place, shut down his whole operation, scared the bejeebers out of him, and ran him off. After that, he never came back.

Okay, he came back, but here's the point. Eddy was able to enter the feed barn because it had a wooden door that was *warped at the bottom*, which was typical of the way this ranch operates most of the time. I don't want to make a big issue out of this and I hate to pass judgment on the guys who work here, but for crying out loud!

If you spend money on sacked feed, put it some place where the coons can't rip up the sacks, because believe me, if they can, they will. Put your feed in a coon-proof barn, and if your barn isn't coon-proof because of a warped door, FIX

THE DOOR!

In a normal world, all of this would be obvious, but those guys aren't normal. We're speaking of Slim and Loper, of course, and you probably figured that out. They're nice guys but careless and...I hate to utter the word, but here we go... they tend to be a little LAZY when it comes to fixing things.

If they would listen to their dogs, we'd have a smooth-running ranch instead of a cheap-john sharecropper operation that's held together with baling wire and duct tape, but they don't listen to their dogs. They don't want to hear our opinions.

However, in this particular situation, that was going to work in my favor, because...did you figure it out? Ha ha. The wooden door into the feed shed was still warped at the bottom and unfixed, which meant that Slim's careless ways had come back to honk him.

He thought he had locked me in the barn? Ha! Guess what. It doesn't do any good to lock the door if it's so warped at the bottom that any dog with half a brain can slither through it.

And for that genius piece of work, ladies and gentlemen, we will give Slim Chance the Duh Award of the Year. See, all I had to do was...

HUH?

Okay, try to stay calm, this is looking bad. I couldn't believe it. Who had...this was an outrage!

Some idiot had plugged the hole with a fifty pound sack of cow feed! Nobody had consulted me or asked my permission. How can I run this ranch when they keep plugging my holes?

I was furious. Okay, he had left me no choice. I would have to destroy the door with blasts of Sonic Boom Barking. When I got finished, they would have two rusty hinges and a pile of toothpick lumber, and I couldn't be held responsible for the damage.

I took a wide stance, pointed the awesome weapon at the door, and began blasting away. Oh, you should have been there to hear it! Fellers, I was pumping 'em out. Two minutes of this kind of high-energy barking will wear out an ordinary dog, and after three minutes, I was bushed. Physically exhausted. Gasping for breath.

Through bleary eyes, I studied the damage and...well, there wasn't any. I mean, the door appeared to be unfazed.

My spirits crashed. I was trapped.

But then...what was that? I heard a voice, a squeaky little voice that seemed to be coming from...well, from nowhere, the sky. It said, "Oh, hi. Noise woke me up."

I jacked myself off the floor and ran my gaze around the interior of the shed. I saw several fifty-pound sacks of feed and some bales of prairie hay, none of which could explain the voice.

A little plume of dust fell from above, slicing through a shaft of sunlight coming from a crack in the door. I lifted my gaze and saw...you're not going to believe this part. I almost couldn't believe it myself.

A raccoon. He was swinging on a ceiling joist, back and forth, did a flip in mid air, grabbed onto another joist, and kept swinging, I mean like a trapeze artist. Then he did a back flip and landed on his feet on the floor beside me.

He looked at me with a grin and said, "Bingo!"

My jaw dropped. "Eddy? Is that you?"

"Yep, same old me. Hi."

"Hi. What are you doing in here? As you very well know, this place is off limits to coons."

"Huh. Forgot." He glanced around and began doing things with his hands. Remember his hands? Always in motion.

"Listen, pal, if someone saw us in here together, it wouldn't help either of our reputations. In fact, I ought to throw the book at you." He reached out his hand and pinched the end of my nose. "Stop that and pay attention. Do you remember who I

am?"

"Sure. Guard dog, bark, stuff like that."

"Eddy, I'm the Head of Ranch Security. One of my main jobs is keeping you and your kinfolks out of this shed. I can't believe you came back. You've put me in a very awkward situation."

"Moonlight Madness. Moon comes out, got to boogie."

"Oh brother!" I began pacing, as I often do when I'm trying to see light at the end of the turnip. "Okay, you haven't done any damage yet. That's good. Nobody has seen us and that's good."

"You want to see a trick?"

"No. Pay attention. You need to get out of here, now. Do you copy?"

"No prob. See you."

"Wait, I forgot, you can't leave."

"How come?"

"Because Slim Chance covered the hole with a fifty-pound sack of feed, that's why."

"Who?"

"Never mind who. The point is that I'm trapped in a secured area with a little crook who's not allowed to be here."

"Huh. Bad deal."

"It's worse than you think. What are we supposed to do, fight to the death?"

"Gosh. Real bad deal."

"I don't like it either, but what else can we do?"

He was sitting on his haunches now. He gave me a grin and whispered behind his hand. "Move the sack."

"Move the sack? Ha ha. It weighs fifty pounds, Shorty. You're Houdini with your hands but you can't lift fifty pounds. Neither can I. And besides, the sack is on the other side of the door, outside the barn. Slim put it there as he was leaving. He plugged the hole and we're cooked."

He grinned and extended his hand. "Bet me?"

"What? Eddy, I haven't had good luck betting against you, and do you know why? Because you're a little con artist, that's why. You always cheat and use sneaky tricks." I paced over to him. "Are you serious?"

"Yep."

"Move the sack?"

"Yep.'

"It can't be done."

"Can."

I heaved a sigh. "Well, buddy, if you've got a trick up your sleeve, give it a shot. I would be amazed and very grateful if you could get us out of here."

"Easy." He monkey-walked over to the door.

I followed, confident that I was going to witness another of his raccoon pranks that were calculated to embarrass the local dog—ME, in other words. He'd done it before, you know, such as the time he lured me into a coon trap by convincing me that it was a helicopter.

I know that sounds crazy, but somehow he did it, and you talk about humiliation! When Slim showed up the next morning...I don't even want to think about it, but the point is that Eddy had a long history of telling gigantic fibs and pulling dirty tricks, so I wasn't expecting much out of this deal.

But you know what? He actually did it! He moved the sack, unplugged the hole, and we were able to resolve the situation without a fight to the death. I sat there and watched the whole thing.

I'm sure you're aching to know how he did it, and I'd love to tell you, but it's classified Top Secret and I don't dare open the files on it. No kidding.

See, there are some parts of this job that we can't share with the general public. I mean, the guy was using a kind of trickery we'd never seen before. Just imagine what would happen if the Bad Guys got wind of it.

Sorry.

CHAPTER EIGHT

I Bust Out of Jail

O h what the heck, maybe it wouldn't hurt, but you have to promise not to blab it around. Don't forget, this is *very* sensitive information.

STAND BY TO VIEW FILE #435-7611

TOP SECRET WITH EXCLAMATION MARK!

SUBJECT: IMPOSSIBLE TASK #356

ANYONE HEARING THIS MESSAGE MUST

BE OVER 76 YEARS OF AGE

Okay, here's the secret file and here's how Eddy did it. He went to the door whose warped opening had been plugged with a sack of feed. He plopped himself down in front of the door and wiggled his hand through the crack. Using his sharp claws, he ripped a hole in the paper sack, then with his amazing little hand, he pulled out a pellet of feed.

He held it up and grinned, to which I said, "So what? One cube. Like I said, it can't be done."

Then he proceeded to empty the entire sack by moving fifty pounds of feed, one cube at a time. I mean, it was the kind of work that ants do. He reached in, brought one out, pitched it over his shoulder, reached in, got another, and kept going. It took half an hour and I almost died of boredom, but by George, he got 'er done.

END OF TOP SECRET FILE
PLEASE DESTROY AT ONCE!
AND EAT YOUR SPINACH!

So there we are. It was such a simple solution, I felt like a dummy that I hadn't thought of it. Actually, it was a simple job for a coon because he had hands and fingers. No dog could have done it, so maybe I shouldn't be too hard on myself.

He pulled out the last cube, held it up, and grinned. "Bingo!" He popped it into his mouth and crunched it up. Then he honked my nose one more time. "Gotta boogie, Abyssinia." He slipped

through the space he had just unplugged and vanished.

It took me a moment to get over the shock. "Hey, Eddy, wait!" I slithered through the crack and came out on the other side. I caught a glimpse of him and...how can I describe the way coons run?

They walk like a monkey, don't you know, but run like a bear, a kind of rollie-polie form of motion. I caught a glimpse of him, rolling along like a little bear, just before he disappeared in some tall weeds near the creek.

"Eddy, thanks, pal! I'm very grateful, but don't ever come back!"

Amazing. If I had laid bets against the little swindler, I would have lost, big-time. He not only had solved a problem that I couldn't have solved, but he had done me a favor in the process. When you deal with coons on a regular basis, you don't expect favors, only mischief.

So, wow, I was a free dog and it was time to get back to the Case of the Wandering Goats. I mean, without me on the job, there was no telling what kind of mess Slim and Deputy Kile might be getting into.

I hit Turbo Five and went roaring off to the east, through ranch headquarters. As I approached the yard, I saw Stub Tail sitting beside the gate with his buddy, the cat. I throttled back just enough to fire off a blistering announcement.

"Drover, we'll start your court martial as soon as I get back, and your weekend pass is cancelled."

"Yeah, but..."

"And Pete, if you see any Aoudad sheep, tell 'em hello for me, okay?"

Hee hee. Kitty had no reply to that slashing remark, I mean, what could he say? He hadn't seen any Aoudad sheep because *there weren't any*. Maybe Palo Duro Canyon had Aoudads, but that was 140 miles to the southwest. We had no exotic animals on my ranch. If we did, I would be the very first to know about it.

I hadn't seen any Aoudads, therefore they didn't exist. It was just another of Kitty's big fat lies. I would settle matters with him as soon as I got Drover's nose in the corner where it belonged. I could hardly wait.

Anyway, I zoomed past the yard, past the house, and onward to the east. Why the east? Because that's where we'd seen the goats crossing the road. They were somewhere along the creek east of headquarters, in a zone that lay between Sally May's house and the big two-story house where Miss Viola lived with her aging parents.

Was it possible that I would be seeing Miss Viola while on this important mission? If so, that was a Big Wow, because she was the cutest, sweetest lady in the whole county, and don't forget, she was crazy about me.

I know, I know, she liked Slim too, and wore his engagement ring with the microscopic diamond, but I was pretty sure that I had played a major role in their engagement. Let's face it. He was a skinny bachelor who ate boiled turkey necks for breakfast and greeted important guests in his drawers.

On his own, Slim would have had a hard time impressing a lady buzzard, much less the Blue Jean Queen of North America. I'm sure you'll agree that there had to be more to this than Slim, and that mysterious something was...well, we might as well go ahead and say it: ME.

Maybe our paths would cross today and she would get to see me at work on a big, important case. Fellers, that was exciting!

But first I had to find the goats. You can't capture missing goats until you find them.

I went north from headquarters, to the mailbox, turned right onto the county road, and headed east in a nice, easy trot. See, I knew this would be a journey of several miles and trotting is the best pace for long trips.

Two miles east of headquarters, I came to Slim's mailbox on the north side of the road. It was a box made of tin that sat on top of a wooden post. I slowed my pace and checked the base of the post for messages. There weren't any, so I left one of my own.

You're probably wondering how I did that, so here's the scoop. I laid down a message with a couple of squirts of invisible ink, and made it short and to the point: "Hank was here. This is my mail box. Buzz off!"

Pretty slick, huh? You bet. I get a kick out of leaving stern messages.

At that point, I thought I heard a voice in the distance, off to the north. I lifted Earatory Scanners and homed in on the sound. Yes, it appeared to be a man's voice, and unless I was mistaken, he shouted, "Nice shot!"

I figured it out. One of the men had roped a goat. It appeared that they had started the job without me, and they were somewhere north of my present location. I needed to join the team before they messed things up.

I kicked up the pace and headed north on the dusty trail that led down to Slim's house, then continued on a northward course, following the creek. At this point in the mission, I was looking for the pickup and stock trailer, not necessarily for goats.

If I located the pickup, the men wouldn't be far away. See, I understood their strategy for this kind of operation: rope the goats, tie them down with a pigging string, come back later with the trailer and load them. In other words, they would be using the stock trailer as a portable catch pen.

How could a dog know all this? Heh. Most dogs don't, but cowdogs do. Hey, this wasn't my first rodeo or my first day on the job. They didn't make me Head of Ranch Security strictly on my good looks...although we can't deny that gasping good looks had played a major part in that decision.

See, in my line of work, you need all sorts of skills, and dashing good looks can come in very handy. They can get you through times when you have no idea what you're doing.

Hmm. That doesn't sound right, so let's move along to something else.

Where were we? Oh yes, out in the wilderness, scouting for cowboys and a pickup-trailer rig. And speaking of wilderness, that country north of Slim's house had a wild and wooly look to it, and a thought popped into my head: "I'm out here, all alone in the wilderness. What if I happened to run into some bloodthirsty coyotes?"

You didn't think of that, did you? Neither did I, but all at once I found myself thinking about it. See, we have coyotes on this ranch, a bunch of them. They look like dogs and sometimes they act like dogs, but they're something different and a little scary.

Take Rip and Snort for example. On a good day, they're a barrel of laughs, the best good-old-boys you ever met. They have studied Goofing Off from every possible angle and have raised it to a science. Any time I have a question about Goofing Off, I know exactly where to go: the coyote brothers.

On the other hand, if they're having a bad day, if they're in a crabby mood, or (this is the big one) if they're *hungry*, a smart dog will go out of his way to avoid them. I call them "cannibals" for a reason. A coyote will eat anything that doesn't eat him first, and when they're hungry, they don't care if lunch might be a distant cousin.

Yes, there had been times when I'd gotten the impression that they might eat me, if they got half a chance.

Gulp.

I stopped and turned my gaze around in a full

circle. You know, sometimes you get the feeling that you're being watched, right? You try to tell yourself, "Oh, I'm just being silly," but then you notice that the hairs on the back of your neck are standing up.

What do hairs know about anything? I don't know, but my years in the Security Business have taught me to pay attention to those hairs on the back of my neck. When they stand up, I get a creepy feeling and I pay attention.

That's where things stood when the shots rang out, I mean, a burst of automatic gunfire. *They were shooting at me with machineguns!*

Bah-ah-ah-ah-ah!

What do you do when they open up with machinegun fire? Bark, run, hit the ground, try to hide? Hey, I couldn't see them and had no idea where they were or who they were. Coyotes? The Charlies? Other enemy agents we didn't know about?

Fellers, I was in serious trouble, so don't quit me now. Keep reading. Please!

CHAPTER NINE

Machinegun Fire!

A re you still with me? I hope so, because this had turned into one of the scariest situations of my whole career—pinned down by a squadron of Charlie Monsters who were blasting away with P-38 automatic weapons, I mean, the bullets were kicking up dirt all around me.

I had just about decided to make a run for it when I saw...huh? Incredible. Who would have thought it?

Ha ha. Never mind. We can call off the Fire Drill. You won't believe this.

Okay, let's take it one step at a time. Remember that blast of machinegun fire? Ha ha. Have you ever heard a goat? They make a sound that is called "bleating." They bleat, making a rapid staccato noise that can easily be mistaken for the sound of an enemy machinegun.

Any dog who'd been alone in the wilderness would have thought he was drawing enemy fire, no kidding. Hey, even I got fooled for a second, until I saw...well, a goat, a white goat with small horns and big floppy ears.

He'd been tied down with a pigging string, don't you see, and suddenly the puddles of the place began falling into pieces. Don't you get it? One of my men, Slim or Deputy Kile, had roped him, tied him down, and left him there while they went looking for more goats. When they got done, they would come back with the trailer and load him up.

I know that we've already covered this, but sometimes you don't pay attention and we have to go over things again. Go ahead and admit it.

But the impointant point is that I hadn't been massacred by the Charlies, and from my perspective, that was the best news of the day. I heaved a huge sigh of relief and tried to get a handle on my trembling legs.

By the way and for the record, the insides of my legs were wet. Apparently we'd spilled some invisible ink during the attack, but it was no big deal.

I hiked over to the goat and took a closer look.

"You sure have big ears, pal. I guess you can't help it, but they make you look silly."

"Bah-ah-ah-ah-ah!"

"Has anyone ever said that you sound like a machinegun?"

"Bah-ah-ah-ah-ah!"

"See what I mean? You scared me out of two years' growth, so try to be more careful. Now, if you'll excuse me, I have work to do."

I turned to leave and...yikes...ran smooth into something big and hairy, two somethings big and hairy, and they had a powerful odor that you'd describe as WILD.

I blinked my eyes, hoping they were playing tricks on me, and stared right into the yellow gaze of two cannibals.

Have you figured it out? Bad news. Rip and Snort, the very guys I really didn't want to meet out there in the wilderness.

My mind tumbled as I searched for something to say that would, uh, break the tension of the moment.

"Hey, Rip and Snort! How's it going, fellas?"

Snort gave me a flat, ugly stare. "That you, Hunk?"

"It is, yes, the same charming fellow you've known for years. I mean, what a great friendship!"

"Pretty dumb for Hunk walk around in wild place, away from house and boom-boom."

"Yes, well, I was out on a stroll. Actually, Snort, I was looking for you boys. Is that a coincidence or what?"

The brothers traded glances and Rip said, "Uh." That's all he ever says. The guy isn't a big talker.

Snort turned back to me and he had a bad look. "How come dummy ranch dog looking for troll in wild place?"

"No, I was out on a *stroll*, a little morning walk, don't you see." He gave me a blank stare, I mean solid granite. "Snort, here's the deal. We've been friends for years and I've never gotten around to telling you that our friendship means a lot, no kidding."

He laughed. "Ha! Coyote eat friendships all time, ho ho!

"It makes me sad to hear you say that."

"Not give a hoot for sad to say. Friendship with coyote not worth kerflooey."

"Well, that's even sadder, because it suggests that our friendship doesn't amount to much. I mean, kerflooey is a tiny unit of measurement. Ten kerflooeys make a drip and ten drips make a drop, and that's just a drop in the bucket."

"Hunk trying for be funny?"

"Well, I…yes, of course, and the reason is that you guys make me nervous when you stare at me like that."

"Ha! Rip and Snort not give a hoot for nervous drip drop."

This was getting scary and I needed to stall for time. "Okay, fine, let's talk about something else. How's the family? The kids are growing up, I guess."

"Kids eat too much, got fleas, make noise all time."

"Well, so much for that. Boy, this weather has been nice, hasn't it?"

"Hunk talk too much."

"Sorry."

"Hunk shut trap."

"Yes sir."

Snort jerked his head toward the goat. "What that's?"

"I beg your pardon?"

"What that's?"

"Oh, you mean 'what is that?'"

"Hunk not know how to talk for phooey. What that's?"

"That is a goat."

He shook his head. "Not look like ghost."

"You're right. It doesn't look like a ghost

because it's a *goat*. Maybe you were thinking about roast goat and got a G in the wrong place, so it came out 'ghost' instead of 'roast'."

The brothers held a conference of whispers, then Snort turned back to me. "Brothers not believe in roast ghost. Must be ship."

"It's a ship? You mean like a boat?"

He was getting angry, I could tell, and he stuck his sharp nose in my face. "Brothers not talk about roast boat. Ship! Bah bah black ship, have so many wool."

"Ohhh, *sheep*! I get it now. You think that's a sheep?"

"Brothers know ship when see ship."

"Sorry, you don't make yourself clear sometimes, and I'm sure you noticed that this particular animal is white, not black." He raised his paw like a hammer. "But who notices color, right?"

"Hunk all time blabber mouth."

"Okay, but let me point out something." I leaned toward him and whispered the message in a soft, sensitive voice, I mean, I didn't want to get him stirred up again. "That's not a sheep. It's a goat."

So much for sensitive. He pushed my face into the dirt. "Hunk shut trap. That ship, not ghost, and brothers eat bah-bah black ship for lunch, oh boy!"

I brushed the dirt off my nose and spitted some out of my mouth. Spat. "One more tiny point, Snort, and I really hate to say this, but that goat...uh, that sheep belongs to the Twitchell Public Schools. It's a show sheep for the children in town. It's not mine to give away. I'm sure you understand."

He scalded me with a flaming glare, then went into another whispering session with his brother. They rumbled and growled, and that made me uneasy, but when they turned back to me, something had changed.

Their faces had softened and maybe for the first time ever, they appeared pleasant and reasonable.

Gee, I guess my presentation had just overwhelmed them, maybe even changed their lives. You know, sometimes I estumunderate my powers of persuasion. I mean, when a dog can present a firm, reasonable argument and turn around the lives of two cannibals, that's pretty amazing.

Snort came toward me and laid a big paw on my shoulder. "Brothers not no more want to eat show ship of little children in town."

"Snort, I'm really touched that you've come

around on this."

"Brothers not even want to eat little children too."

"That is so sweet! It almost brings tears to my eyes, no kidding."

He turned his gaze toward the sky. "Rip and Snort decide to eat dummy ranch dog instead."

"Dummy ranch dog?"

His gaze drifted down to me, and he flashed a toothy grin that looked like a bear trap. "Brothers make big yum-yum out of Hunk, oh boy!"

"What!" Now they were both staring at me with glittering yellow eyes, and licking their chops. I took a step backward. "What about our friendship?"

"Ha! Kerflooey."

"Kerflooey? Is that all you can say? What about the great times we've had? Remember the night we ate silage and sang all night?"

"Kerflooey."

I took another step backward. "Okay, Snort, we're down to the basics, the place where we go when we have to make our most difficult decisions. I want you...I want you and Rip to think about the Brotherhood of All Dogs. See, eating your kinfolks is just WRONG, Snort. There has to be a better way of settling arguments."

This brought a chorus of rude laughter and I

knew I was in big trouble.

"All right, you leave me no choice. I must tell you that I'm a black belt in kerflooey." Oops. They roared with laughter. "I meant karate, and I'm serious. These paws are registered as Deadly Weapons."

More irreverent laughter. Rip was laughing so hard, he fell over and started kicking his legs. Snort was staggering with laughter. Well, this wasn't going according to plan, and the conditions seemed right for me to make a run for it.

I turned, hit Full Turbos, and went streaking toward the...BAM...those guys aren't as dumb as they look, and a lot faster than you'd think. In mere seconds, their laughter vanished and they decked me after I'd gone five steps. I went to the ground and they were on top of me.

Well, I guess that's about it. There's no way this will ever work out, and you know how I am about the little children. They shouldn't be hearing cannibal stories at bedtime, not the ones that are true to life, so let's just shut everything down and send them off to bed, okay?

If you have the courage to hear the rest of this story, I guess you can go on to the next chapter, but I can't make any promises about how it'll turn out.

I Meet King Aouda

You're still with me? Good, I was worried about that, because we're heading straight into the Scary Part. Get a firm grip on something stout and we'll see what happens.

Okay, there I was, at the bottom of a pile of hungry cannibals, and fellers, things were looking bad. The good news is that they didn't eat me right away. Instead, they did something that would seem strange to anyone but a cannibal: while sitting on top of me, they sat up proud and sang their Sacred Hymn and National Anthemum.

> Me just a worthless coyote,
> Me howling at the moon.
> Me like to sing and holler.

Me crazy as a loon.

Me not want job or duties,
No church or Sunday school.
Me just a worthless coyote,
But me ain't nobody's fool.

Remember that song? Over the years, I had heard them sing it many times. It never got any better and remained a tuneless little piece of coyote trash. By the way, even though Rip never talked, he could sing and he sang his cannibal heart out—if he had a heart, and I wouldn't swear to that.

When they got finished with the so-called "singing," they broke into a chorus of blood-chilling yips and screeches, and Snort yelled, "Rip and Snort better singests in whole world, sing so wummerful, even big rocks cry!"

Rip added his opinion. "Uh!"

"Now brothers make big yum-yum feast with dummy ranch dog. Snort got first dibs on drumstick, oh boy!"

Oh boy? Oh brother. I was in deepest trouble and this time there was no way out, no magic pullet. Bullet, that is. A pullet is a kind of chicken, slurp, so let's back up and try it again.

There was no magic *bullet* to save my bakery. To save my *bacon*.

As you can see, I was pretty shook up. It looked hopeless. The brothers were hooting and screeching and jumping up and down on my potsrate body, but then all of a sudden, we heard...what was that? Some kind of singing?

The brothers stopped their noise-making and stopped jumping up and down on my back. I heard a loud grunt from Rip, then Snort said, "What that's coming from trees and butches?"

I squirmed out from under the big lugs, and we all sat very still and listened. Here's what we heard, a chorus of invisible voices.

He is Aouda, Aouda Abudai!
King of all below the shining sky.
From rugged Atlas Mountains we have roamed.
Ancient Carthage is our home!

Wow, this was really strange. I mean, we were hearing chanting voices coming from somewhere, yet we couldn't see anyone or anything that might have been the source.

Then...they appeared! We saw them marching in single file out of the bushes along the creek

(Snort had called them "butches," remember?), the bushes along the creek, and you talk about getting a case of the CREEPS! The hair on the back of my neck shot up. My eyes bugged out and electricity crackled down my backbone and went out to the end of my tail, where it fried a clump of hair.

No kidding, *fried* it.

Here's what we saw: seven creatures unknown to us. They were tan in color, bigger than coyotes, bigger than mule deer, but smaller than cows or horses. They wore huge curled horns on their heads and each had a shaggy mane or beard flowing down the front of its neck.

They resembled sheep or goats, but unlike any sheep or goats I'd ever seen.

Rip and Snort weren't afraid of anything, but this procession of strange animals got their attention. In fact, I got the impression that they were as spooked as I was.

Snort leaned toward me. "What that's coming?"

"I have no idea."

"Hunk rutch out and beat 'em up."

"Are you nuts? You can forget that, pal. I want no part of those horns." I took a closer look. "Wait a second. You know what? *Those might be Aoudad sheep!*"

"Howbad ship?"

"Exactly. I've had them under surveillance for weeks."

"Uh. Howbad ships look too tough for mess around with."

"My thoughts exactly."

The brothers took up a position behind me. In other words, they put ME between themselves and the Aoudads, and Snort growled, "Hunk beat 'em up or brothers break face."

"You beat 'em up! You're the tough guys around here."

Snort didn't argue. You know what he did? He and his thuggish brother put their shoulders into my back and began pushing me toward the strangers. I tried to dig my claws into the ground, but it was like trying to resist a couple of trucks.

Gulp.

The Aoudad procession marched up to us and stopped. The leader, the one out front, was the biggest of the bunch. He had huge horns, a flowing beard, and weird yellow-green eyes.

He stared at us, made a grunting sound, stamped his foot, and stepped toward me. "I am Aouda! Aouda Abudai! I am the reever that fids my sheeple!" (Translation: "I am the river that feeds my people.")

The fearsome cannibal brothers cowered behind me, as still as statues, didn't move a hair or make a squeak. Aouda tramped over to the goat that was hogtied on the ground, looked him over, and marched back to us.

"Who amongst you ees going to itt theese leetle gut?" (Translation: "Who among you is going to eat this little goat?") His stern amber gaze swept over us. Rip and Snort shrank down, shook their heads, and pointed at ME!

Aouda moved closer, until our noses were almost touching. I caught a whiff of him now. He STUNK, but I wasn't about to bring it up.

In a low rumbling voice, he said, "Duggie wish to itt theese poor leetle gut?" (Translation: "Doggie wish to eat this poor little goat?")

My mouth had become very dry and I swallowed hard. "Oh no sir, not me. In fact, I'm I'm I'm the the the the Head of Ranch Security."

"I dunt care who you are."

"Yes, but my point is...and this is crucial...my point is that I answered a distress call this morning and tried to rescue this poor, helpless little goat." I whirled around and pointed straight at the brothers. "And found these two heartless ruffians lurking around him!"

Snort flinched and grumbled, "Hunk shut

trap!"

I ignored him and plunged on. "They're coyotes, Aouda. You know who eats poor little goats around here? Coyotes! And you know what else? When you came marching out of the brush, Snort said that y'all stink!"

Aouda chuckled. "I dunt care what anyone say about stink."

"Yes, but then Snort said he was going to beat the everlasting snot out of you."

The big guy seemed puzzled by this. "And what does theese mean, bit snot out of?"

"Snort thinks you're just a bunch of sissy sheep."

He smiled. "That ees incorrect. Bad information."

"I agree, and that's what I tried to tell him, but coyotes think they can whip anything on four legs."

Aouda smiled. "Not everything."

He turned and walked a few steps away, toward a medium-sized hackberry tree. Five feet away from it, he stopped, lowered his head, and pawed up some dirt. In a split second, he rocked back on his hind legs, exploded out of his tracks, and rammed it.

WHAM!

The tree didn't break in half, but it shuddered and dropped a bunch of branches and leaves.

Then he stood on his back legs and began slashing the bark off the trunk with his front hooves. Fellers, that was no small deal, because hackberry bark is as tough as it gets.

Rip and Snort watched with wide eyes.

Aouda returned to us, wearing a little grin. He spoke to Snort. "You want bit snot out of Aouda?" Snort shook his head. Aouda jerked his head toward his six warriors who appeared ready to whomp up on someone. "Them?" Snort shook his head. Aouda looked at Rip. "You?" Rip shook his head. "Then be gone!"

This was amazing. The ferocious cannibal brothers went slinking away, and we're talking about naughty boys who'd been caught stealing cookies. I was tempted to stand up and cheer and…okay, let's be truthful. I felt a powerful urge talk some trash about how they'd better think twice about messing with the Head of Ranch Security, but I managed to hold it back.

The brothers vanished into the brush along the creek, and I found myself standing alone beside this big dude who called himself Aouda. "That was a nice piece of work, Your Majesty."

"Eet was nothing." He moved closer and whispered in my ear. "Do not harm leetle gut."

"Yes sir. We'll take him back to his home,

honest."

"Good."

King Aouda returned to his column of warriors and they marched away, singing their song again.

He is Aouda, Aouda Abudai!
King of all below the shining sky.
From rugged Atlas Mountains we have roamed.
Ancient Carthage is our home!

Roping Fools

Is that incredible or what? In the space of a few minutes, I had been beat up, beat down, beaten all around, yet here I was, alive and alone in the wilderness with a little white goat.

Everyone had gone. I was safe and alive to fight another day!

I didn't have time to faint with relief because fainting wasn't an option. Don't forget, cannibals are bad about holding a grudge, and I needed to move along.

I went over to the goat, who was still hog-tied. "Okay, bud, just relax and enjoy the morning air. We'll be back to fetch you in a bit and take you home."

"Bah-ah-ah-ah-ah!"

95

Do you speak Goat? If not, here is the translation of what he said: "Oh Hank, you are such a hero, such a brave and noble dog! I can't believe you whipped those coyotes all by yourself! Thank you, thank you!"

You know, goats have a kind of brainless expression, but they're smarter than you might suppose.

Anyway, it was time for me to get back to work. I left the goat and headed north, down the creek, to look for my cowboy pals. I had gone about half a mile when I came upon the pickup and trailer. The trailer was empty, which allowed me to pile up some important clues:

1. There were no horses inside, and maybe that's obvious. I mean, "empty trailer" means "no horses," so let's move along.
2. There were no goats in the trailer either, an indication that...
3. The boys weren't having much luck roping goats.
4. This came as no surprise, because...
5. They were trying to do the job without a dog...
6. Because they had locked me in the feed barn and...
7. How dumb was that?
8. That's the end of the Clue List.

Off in the distance, I heard the thunder of hooves and the crashing of brush, so I cranked up the jets and headed toward the sounds, to a clearing on the north side of the creek.

Up ahead, I saw the drama unfoliating. Unfolding, I guess it should be, the drama unfolding, and it looked pretty dramatic. Chief Deputy Kile was in hot pursuit of a goat that was running wide open and dodging like a jackrabbit. Slim galloped along behind, carrying a loaded rope.

The deputy stood up in his stirrups, swung his twine, and made his throw. It went straight to the mark, but the goat ran through the loop and kept trucking.

Slim laughed. "You might try jerking your slack!"

"I did jerk my slack!"

"Don't matter, it's still a miss."

"If you're so smart, show me how it's done!"

"Stand by and study your lessons!"

Mind you, they were having this conversation in a full gallop while pursuing the goat.

Deputy Kile pulled out of the chase and Slim took his place, and he had old Snips running wide open—neck stretched out, mane flapping in the breeze, and all four feet throwing up grass and dirt. Slim lined out his shot, stood up in the stirrups, raised a small goat-sized loop above his head, and started his twirl.

This was looking so good, I cut loose with some Motivational Barks. "Good position! Give the loop a little spin to the left so that it'll hang on his neck, and be quick about grabbing slack! Got that? Jerk slack and dally!"

You wouldn't expect a dog to know so much about roping, would you? Heh. Most dogs don't, and we can use Drover as a perfect example. The runt knows nothing about roping, because he never goes with the guys when they're doctoring calves in the pasture.

He's either asleep on his gunny sack bed or whispering gossip with the local cat, so his knowledge of roping amounts to a big fat goose egg. Zero.

Actually, he knows one thing about roping. He knows that when Slim Chance is horseback and holding a loop, a dog needs to stay *behind* the horse. Why? Because Slim is such a goof-off, he will never pass up a chance to rope an unsuspecting dog.

It happened only once to Stub Tail. He was trotting along beside Slim's horse, on the right side. Slim flipped out a Hoolihan loop and nailed him, and it never happened again. Now, when Drover sees a loaded rope, he heads for the machine shed. He is such a little chicken liver.

Oh well.

Where were we? Oh yes, Sally May's rotten, pampered, scheming little crook of a cat. He had told me a pack of lies about seeing Aoudad sheep, remember? Well, maybe he actually *had* seen them, but that just goes to show what a sneak he is. Sometimes he tells the truth to throw us off balance, and that's cheating in a different set of clothes.

But we weren't talking about the cat. We were roping goats and you need to start paying attention.

Okay, Slim was hot on the tail of a squirmy, dodgy little goat, and things were looking pretty good, but who could have predicted that the goat would run smooth over the top of a wild turkey hen that was sitting on her nest of eggs?

That's one of those random events you don't expect in the midst of a goat-roping adventure.

Guess what happens when you disturb a nesting turkey. She takes off like a helicopter. And guess how your average ranch horse reacts to a helicopter right in front of his nose.

Wow.

Old Snips went bug-eyed and started bucking. Slim lost his rope and one rein, and started grabbing leather. Deputy Kile saw a wreck-in-

the-making and galloped toward the horse. I suppose he planned to grab the loose rein to keep Snips from bucking into the trees along the creek, but he was a little late and, well, Slim ate one. A tree, that is.

It wasn't a huge tree with the kind of big limbs that could do serious damage, just a half-grown cedar, but it was big enough to sweep him out of the saddle and land him tail-first on the ground.

KA-BAM!

Well, you know me. When my guys get busted in the pasture, I hit Sirens and Lights and head for the crash scene. A lot of dogs wouldn't bother, because they don't care. You know who cares? Cowdogs.

By the time I pulled up with lights flashing, Deputy Kile was already on the ground, kneeling beside him. I went straight to my pal and...

"Hank, move!"

...and decided to postpone the CPR Licks on the Face. I mean, Deputy Kile was trained in first aid, so I let him take the lead on this. I knew he would call me if he got in over his head.

He looked into Slim's face. "Can you tell how bad you're hurt?" Slim shook his head. "Any pain in the neck?" Slim pointed...well, he seemed to be pointing...was he pointing at ME? Was that some kind of joke? "Slim does your neck hurt?"

"No."

"Head? Back?"

"My tail hurts."

"Well, that's serious. You could have brain damage."

"Bobby, you keep trying to be funny, but you still ain't. Help me up."

"Just lie still and let's check things out."

"I'm lying in a red ant den and they're crawling on me."

"Well, if you're worried about ants, I guess you're not hurt too bad."

The deputy stood up, offered a hand, and hoisted him up off the ground. Slim took a few steps and looked like an old man, bent over and shuffling along. Deputy Kile was watching. "How does it feel?"

"Well, it hurts. I landed on it, hard."

"You need to see a doctor?"

"No. What would he do, amputate my hiney?"

"Can you ride?"

Slim shuffled around some more. "I don't think so. I'm not even sure I'll want to drive a pickup. This thing hurts."

Deputy Kile pressed his lips together and

gave his head a sad shake. "I can't imagine something like this happening to Roy and Gene."

"Bobby, you need to stop watching cowboy movies and move back to the real world. You might actually learn something."

"I know, but it's so sad, the way standards have declined."

Slim shook his head and muttered under his breath. He removed his hat and wiped his forehead on the sleeve of his shirt. "I'm out of the lineup. You'll have to catch the other eleven yourself. The way you rope, it'll take two and a half months."

The deputy's smile faded. "Yeah, it's like trying to catch rabbits."

"Well, if you spent more time practicing your throws, and less time mouthing off about Roy and Gene, you'd be a roper instead of a hoper."

The deputy scuffed up some dirt with his boot. "Maybe we should have tried calling those goats with feed, instead of roping."

"Fine time for you to think of that."

"Well, you were hot to do it the Cowboy Way."

"Bobby, you're the one who brought it up in the first place. I was sitting in my house, eating my breakfast, and minding my own business. Now here I am, crippled."

There was a long silence, then the deputy said, "I can't catch those goats by myself. What are we going to do?"

Slim shrugged. "I guess we could put out the word amongst the local coyotes that we brung 'em some lunch."

It looked like the end of the road, but then... you'll never guess what happened next, so you'd better keep reading.

Pretty amazing.

CHAPTER TWELVE

I Rescue the Goats

Okay, the roping adventure had gone south and ended in failure. My so-called cowboys had spent half the morning chasing goats around the ranch and had managed to catch one out of twelve. Worse still, Slim had injured his hiney and couldn't sit on a horse.

In other words, this was a typical cowboy deal.

You'd think they might have put me into the game and let me clean up their mess, I mean, what's the point of having a top-of-the-line, blue ribbon cowdog on the ranch if you don't use him?

And don't forget, I had saved the one goat they'd managed to catch—not only saved him from the cannibal brothers, but also from a tribe of goat-eating Aoudads.

Don't get me started on this. The sad truth is that our people don't want to hear what the dogs think and won't give us a chance to show our stuff. Fine. Rip and Snort would be happy to hear that they had plenty of sandwich meat for the rest of the week.

But just then, we heard...what was that, a horn honking? Yes, that's what it was, a horn honking in the distance, and suddenly the clues rushed into a pattern. Remember those Aoudad sheep? They had huge horns, right? Don't you get it? Those Aoudads were out there, honking their...

Wait, hold everything. Skip the Aoudads. A pickup drove into view. It was pulling a stock trailer and the driver was honking the horn.

Ha ha. Simple mistake, and forget what I said about the Aoudads. They have nice horns but their horns don't *honk* and they didn't fool me, not even for a second. Pickups have horns that honk.

Slim turned and looked. "Who in the cat hair is that?"

The deputy squinted his eyes. "I don't know, unless...it's Woodrow."

Slim's eyes rolled up in his head. "Oh wonderful, as if things weren't bad enough."

We all studied the situation. The pickup stopped in a little clearing north of the creek. An old man with white hair got out. He wore khaki pants held up with a pair of red suspenders, and no hat. (I noticed and memorized all these little clues. You never know which one will break the case wide open.)

He walked to the back of the stock trailer and opened the gate. Someone else got out on the other side and joined him. The two of them carried something out of the trailer...a portable corral panel. They got another one and another one, and hooked them together, until they had a little catch pen.

The second person appeared to be a woman wearing jeans and red boots, and her hair was pulled back in a ponytail. Holy smokes, that was Miss Viola!

Deputy Kile said, "Should we go help 'em?"

"No, let's see how it plays out."

The old man—that must have been Woodrow, her daddy—got back into the pickup and blew the horn. Viola got a half-sack of feed out of the back of the pickup and started walking to the west, away from the pickup.

She stopped, rattled the sack, and made a soft sound. "Wooooo! Come on, feed, come on!" She turned and started walking back toward the portable pen, rattling the sack and making her call.

All of us were watching. A bunch of white creatures came prancing out of the brush along the creek. They had big floppy ears and they moved like minnows, following the one in the lead. Holy smokes, they were goats!

Deputy Kile said, "Will you look at that!"

"Did you get a count?"

"Eleven head."

"Good honk."

Miss Viola entered the little pen and started scattering feed pellets on the ground. The lead goat lifted its head and sniffed. The others stopped and sniffed, then the lead goat trotted into the pen, dropped its head, and started eating. The others scrambled into the pen and started eating too.

Viola took slow, careful steps to the opening, dragged one of the panels and closed the pen. She had just penned eleven head of goats.

Slim was smiling. "By grabs, she done it! I wouldn't have bet a nickel on it."

Slim caught his horse and we walked over to Woodrow's pickup. I took my place, walking beside Slim to give him some encouragement. I mean, the guy looked pitiful, all bent over and walking like a turkey.

Woodrow got out of the pickup and hooked his thumbs into his suspenders. He watched us with smoky gray eyes that peered out below shaggy eyebrows, and as usual, he looked grouchy.

In a gruff voice, he said, "We penned your goats."

Slim said, "Thanks, Woodrow."

"That hot-rod cowboy stuff is fun, but you can get a lot more done with a sack of feed. It's easier to *pull* a string than to push it."

"Thanks, Woodrow."

"Somebody left a goat tied down."

"That was me."

"We took care of that mess too. He's in the trailer."

"Thanks, Woodrow."

Viola had noticed Slim's limp and came toward him. Or was she coming to ME? Yes, of course, she was crazy about me, remember? I quit Slim and dashed out to...she walked right past me and went to Slim.

Rats.

He said, "That was a nice piece of ranch work, penning those goats."

"Thank you. What's wrong? You're walking funny."

"My pride got hurt."

She gave him a hard look—and fellers, she could do that pretty well, squinting one eye, raising the other eyebrow, and pinching her lips. "Slim, what's wrong? I've got eyes."

"I got unhorsed, if you must know, and landed where the sun don't shine."

"Do you need a doctor?"

"I need a psychiatrist for hanging out with riff-raff." He jerked a thumb toward Deputy Kile. He barked a laugh.

Viola didn't smile. "I'll be glad to take you to the doctor."

"I ain't going to the doctor. All he knows to do is stick you with needles."

"All right, the chiropractor."

"I don't like him either."

She shook her head. "You're hopeless." Her gaze drifted around and landed on me (finally), and she smiled a smile that lit up the whole world. "Hi, Hank."

Did you hear that? Wow, she sure had a gift with words, I mean, it was like hearing a love poem. I told you she loved me ten times more than she loved Slim! My heart went to clanging and banging around in my chest, and I was so overcome by the beauty of her words, I did something truly amazing.

You might find this hard to believe, but I did it, honest, and here's what I did. From a standing position, and we're talking about all four paws on the ground, no running start or warm-up, I leaped straight into her arms.

Show me another dog who could do that. Drover might have made it to knee-level. Me? I landed in her arms, ABOVE HER WAIST, and lit with such gusto, she staggered backwards.

Naturally, Slim tried to butt in. "Hank, for crying out loud, leave her alone!"

He tried to tear me out of her loving embrace. but I pressed myself against her and she held me tight and said—you'll like this part—she said, "He likes me."

"Well, so do I!"

She gave him a cute little smirk. "Are you jealous?"

"I didn't know I had to compete with a frazzling dog."

"You never know, mister." She turned her adoring gaze on me. "Hank, you're a sweetie."

Did you hear that? I was her Sweetie!

"But I have to put you down."

What? No! We could run away to Amarillo, rent a castle, and live happy ever-afterly. Forget

Slim!

Bummer. She set me down, slid her hand into the crook of Slim's arm, and gave him one of her sun-up-in-the-morning smiles. "The competition out here is pretty tough. I guess you need to stay alert."

He chuckled. "This world's in a sorry state when a man can't trust his own dog."

Sigh. He got her back and I got a broken heart out of the deal. Oh well. As I've said many times before...I don't remember what I've said many times before, but the point is, we have to trudge on with our lives.

Slim and Deputy Kile loaded their horses into the trailer, and we took both rigs to ranch headquarters. Slim's tail section was hurting and he didn't want to drive, so he stretched out in the bed of the pickup.

I wanted to ride in the cab with Miss Viola and sit in her lap, but her grumpy old daddy said I smelled bad (lies) and wouldn't allow it, so I ended up riding in the back of the pickup with Slim.

He didn't deserve my company and I snubbed him, didn't even look at him. He must have noticed. "Hank, don't get your nose out of joint. You're just a dog."

Just a dog? Is that all he could say? For his

information...phooey.

That's about all the story. Deputy Kile delivered the goats to the ag teacher in Twitchell, and Miss Viola and her daddy went back home. Slim was crippled up for a week with his wounded tailbone and had to do a lot of standing up. In the secret darkness of my heart, I laughed like crazy. It served him right for stealing my girlfriend.

Oh, a couple of details before we wrap up this case. During the lunch hour, I tracked down the King of Slackers and got his court martial out of the way. He spent an entire hour with his nose in the corner.

But here's the best part. After lunch, along about two o'clock, Loper and Little Alfred went off to check windmills. Sally May and Baby Molly went down for a nap, and a deep, mysterious silence spread across ranch headquarters: no prying eyes, no listening ears, no Sally May, and no broom.

Can you guess what might have happened next? Hee hee. I slithered my bad self over the yard fence, caught her rotten little cat napping in the iris patch, woke him up with Train Horns, and ran him up a tree.

Truth and Justice had won another victory, and this case is...

Okay, maybe the little sneak was right about the Aoudad sheep, but nobody needs to know. The record will show that he was misquoted and that I discovered the Aoudads all by myself. That's the Official Story, so keep your trap shut.

Anyway, I rescued the goats and parked Kitty in a tree, and that's as good as it gets. This case is closed.

Have you read all of Hank's adventures?

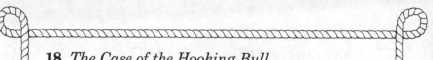

Join Hank the Cowdog's Security Force

Are you a big Hank the Cowdog fan? Then you'll want to join Hank's Security Force! Here is some of the neat stuff you will receive:

Welcome Package
- A Hank paperback
- An Original (19"x25") Hank Poster
- A Hank bookmark

Eight digital issues of *The Hank Times* with
- Lots of great games and puzzles
- Stories about Hank and his friends
- Special previews of future books
- Fun contests

More Security Force Benefits
- Special discounts on Hank books, audios, and more
- Special Members-Only section on website

Total value of the Welcome Package and *The Hank Times* is $23.99. However, your two-year membership is **only $7.99** plus $5.00 for shipping and handling.

☐ Yes I want to join Hank's Security Force. Enclosed is $12.99 ($7.99 + $5.00 for shipping and handling) for my **two-year membership**. [Make check payable to Maverick Books.]

Which book would you like to receive in your Welcome Package? (#   ) any book except #50

_____

BOY or GIRL

YOUR NAME   (CIRCLE ONE)

_____

MAILING ADDRESS

_____

CITY   STATE   ZIP

_____

TELEPHONE   BIRTH DATE

_____

E-MAIL   (required for digital Hank Times)

Send check or money order for $12.99 to:

Hank's Security Force
Maverick Books
PO Box 549
Perryton, Texas 79070

DO NOT SEND CASH. NO CREDIT CARDS ACCEPTED.
Allow 2–3 weeks for delivery.
Offer is subject to change.

The following activities are samples from *The Hank Times*, the official newspaper of Hank's Security Force. Please do not write on these pages unless this is your book. Even then, why not just find a scrap of paper?

"Photogenic"
Memory Quiz #1

We all know that Hank has a "photogenic" memory—being aware of your surroundings is an important quality for a Head of Ranch Security. Now *you* can test your powers of observation.

How good is your memory? Look at the illustration on page 12 and try to remember as many things about it as possible. Then turn back to this page and see how many questions you can answer.

1. How many people are in the wall picture? 1, 2, or 3?

2. Could you see Hank's tongue? Yes or No?

3. How many spiders were there?
   1, 2, 3, or "what spiders"?

4. Which of Hank's ears was higher?
   HIS Left or HIS Right?

5. Were the "BAM"s coming
   from the Window,
   Wall, or Door?

6. How many of Hank's eyes
   could you see? 0, 1, 2, or all 3?

"Word Maker"

Try making up to twenty words from the letters in the name below. Use as many letters as possible, however, don't just add an "s" to a word you've already listed in order to have it count as another. Try to make up entirely new words for each line!

Then, count the total number of letters used in all of the words you made, and see how well you did using the Security Force Rankings below!

DEPUTY   KILE

_____	_____
_____	_____
_____	_____
_____	_____
_____	_____
_____	_____
_____	_____
_____	_____
_____	_____
_____	_____

59-61   You spend too much time with J.T. Cluck and the chickens.

62-64   You are showing some real Security Force potential.

65-68   You have earned a spot on our ranch security team.

69+   Wow! You rank up there as a top-of-the-line cowdog.

"Photogenic" Memory Quiz #2

We all know that Hank has a "photogenic" memory—being aware of your surroundings is an important quality for a Head of Ranch Security. Now you can test your powers of observation.

How good is your memory? Look at the illustration on page 26 and try to remember as many things about it as possible. Then turn back to this page and see how many questions you can answer.

1. What was in the bowl on the table? Fish, Flowers, or Plants?

2. How many drawers were on the dresser? 1, 2, 3, or 4?

3. Did Slim's boots have spurs? Yes or No?

4. How many things were on top of the dresser? 1, 2, 3, or 4?

5. Was Slim pulling on HIS Left or HIS Right boot?

6. How many dogs' eyes could you see? 2, 3, 4, 5, or all 6?

"Rhyme Time"

W hat if the goats decide that they want to leave the ranch and go in search of other jobs? What kinds of jobs could they find?

Make a rhyme using GOATS that would relate to their new job possibilities.

> Example: The GOATS could help people document their research for English class research papers.
> Answer: Goats FOOTNOTES

1. The GOATS could write slips for school saying that you missed the day before because of a doctor's appointment.

2. The GOATS could say clever things that people then want to share with each other.

3. The GOATS rent oars needed to help people make a water craft move.

4. The GOATS pass out life preservers to cruise ships passengers if the ship is sinking.

5. The GOATS make these small bags for carrying things around in.

6. The GOATS grow this crop and make cereal and bran muffins with it.

7. The GOATS make and sell these floating homes.

8. The GOATS dig these around castles.

Answers:

1. Goats NOTES
2. Goats QUOTES
3. Goats ROWBOATS
4. Goats FLOATS
5. Goats TOTES
6. Goats OATS
7. Goats HOUSEBOATS
8. Goats MOATS

Have you visited Hank's official website yet?

www.hankthecowdog.com

Don't miss out on exciting *Hank the Cowdog* games and activities, as well as up-to-date news about upcoming books in the series!

When you visit, you'll find:

- Hank's BLOG, which is updated regularly and is always the first place we announce upcoming books and new products!
- Hank's Official Shop, with tons of great Hank the Cowdog books, audiobooks, games, t-shirts, stuffed animals, mugs, bags, and more!
- Links to Hank's social media, whereby Hank sends out his "Cowdog Wisdom" to fans
- A FREE, printable Map of Hank's Ranch!
- Hank's Music Page where you can listen to songs and even download FREE ringtones!
- A way to sign up for Hank's free email updates
- Sally May's Ranch Round-up Recipes!
- Printable & Colorable Greeting Cards for Holidays
- Articles about Hank and author, John R. Erickson in the news

...AND MUCH, MUCH MORE!

BOOKS
The Collection

FAN ZONE
Fun & Games

AUTHOR
Meet the Creator

STORE
Books & More

Find Toys, Games, Books & More
at the Hank shop.

ANNOUNCING:
A sneak peek at Hank #66

Ever thought of having a Hank the Cowdog-themed Party?

Hank Plays Cupid:

GAMES
COME PLAY WITH HANK & PALS

BOOKS
BROWSE THE ENTIRE HANK CATALOG

FRIENDS
GET TO KNOW THE RANCH GANG

 Visit Hank's Facebook page

 Follow Hank on Twitter

 Watch Hank on YouTube

 Follow Hank on Pinterest

 Send Hank an Email

FROM THE BLOG

JAN 26 Hank is Cupid in Disguise...

JAN 18 The Valentine's Day Robbery! - a Snippet from the Story

DEC 04 Getting SIGNED Hank the Cowdog books for Christmas!

OCT 14 Education Association's lists of recommended books?

VISIT THE BLOG

Hank's Survey
We'd love to know what you think! GO

Hank's Music
Free ringtones, music and more!

MORE

Get the Latest

Keep up with Hank's news and promotions by signing up for our e-news.

Looking for The Hank Times fan club newsletter?

Enter your email address

SIGN UP

TEACHER'S CORNER

Download fun activity guides, discussion questions and more.

Official Shop
Find books, audio, toys and more!

LET'S GO

SALLY MAY'S RECIPES

 Discover delicious recipes from Sally May herself. GO

Join Hank's Security Force
Get the activity letter and other cool stuff.

JOIN   SECURITY FORCE

Hank in the News

 Find out what the media is saying about Hank.

GO

FEATURED BOOK

The Christmas Turkey Disaster

Now Available!

Hank is in real trouble this time. L...

BUY READ LISTEN

BOOKS
Browse Titles
Buy Books
Audio Samples
Other Books

FAN ZONE
Games
Hank & Friends
Security Force
Educational Stuff

AUTHOR
John Erickson's Bio
Hank in the News
In Concert
Contact John

SHOP
The Books
Store
Get Help
Retailer Info

And, be sure to check out the Audiobooks!

If you've never heard a *Hank the Cowdog* audiobook, you're missing out on a lot of fun! Each Hank book has also been recorded as an unabridged audiobook for the whole family to enjoy!

Praise for the Hank Audiobooks:

"It's about time the Lone Star State stopped hogging Hank the Cowdog, the hilarious adventure series about a crime solving ranch dog. Ostensibly for children, the audio renditions by author John R. Erickson are sure to build a cult following among adults as well." — *Parade Magazine*

"Full of regional humor . . . vocals are suitably poignant and ridiculous. A wonderful yarn." — *Booklist*

"For the detectin' and protectin' exploits of the canine Mike Hammer, hang Hank's name right up there with those of other anthropomorphic greats...But there's no sentimentality in Hank: he's just plain more rip-roaring fun than the others. Hank's misadventures as head of ranch security on a spread somewhere in the Texas Panhandle are marvelous situation comedy." — *School Library Journal*

"Knee-slapping funny and gets kids reading."

— *Fort Worth Star Telegram*

Love Hank's Hilarious Songs?

Hank the Cowdog's "Greatest Hits" albums bring together the music from the unabridged audiobooks you know and love! These wonderful collections of hilarious (and sometimes touching) songs are unmatched. Where else can you learn about coyote philosophy, buzzard lore, why your dog is protecting an old corncob, how bugs compare to hot dog buns, and much more!

And, be sure to visit Hank's "Music Page" on the official website to listen to some of the songs and download FREE Hank the Cowdog ringtones!

"Audio-Only" Stories

Ever wondered what those "Audio-Only" Stories in Hank's Official Store are all about? The Audio-Only Stories are *Hank the Cowdog* adventures that have never been released as books. They are about half the length of a typical *Hank* book, and there are currently seven of them. They have run as serial stories in newspapers for years and are now available as audiobooks!

Teacher's Corner

Know a teacher who uses Hank in their classroom? You'll want to be sure they know about Hank's "Teacher's Corner"! Just click on the link on the homepage, and you'll find free teacher's aids, such as a printable map of Hank's ranch, a reading log, coloring pages, blog posts specifically for teachers and librarians, and much more!

John R. Erickson, a former cowboy, has written numerous books for both children and adults and is best known for his acclaimed *Hank the Cowdog* series. The *Hank* series began as a self-publishing venture in Erickson's garage in 1982 and has endured to become one of the nation's most popular series for children and families. Through the eyes of Hank the Cowdog, a smelly, smart-aleck Head of Ranch Security, Erickson gives readers a glimpse into daily life on a cattle ranch in the West Texas Panhandle. His stories have won a number of awards, including the Audie, Oppenheimer, Wrangler, and Lamplighter Awards, and have been translated into Spanish, Danish, Farsi, and Chinese. USA Today calls the *Hank the Cowdog* books "the best family entertainment in years." Erickson lives and works on his ranch in Perryton, Texas, with his family.

Gerald L. Holmes is a largely self-taught artist who grew up on a ranch in Oklahoma. He has illustrated the *Hank the Cowdog* books and serial stories, in addition to numerous other cartoons and textbooks, for over thirty years, and his paintings have been featured in various galleries across the United States. He and his wife live in Perryton, Texas, where they raised their family, and where he continues to

paint his wonderfully funny and accurate portrayals of modern American ranch life to this day.